DAISY GOES TO THE RACES

Book One: The Daisy Starshine Series

Mark W. Stevens

THIRD MOUNTAIN PUBLISHING

Illustrations by Mark W. Stevens

Cover design by Waleed Rabin

This book is dedicated to my granddaughter, Helena, who was my inspiration for this story. There is a little bit of her in each of my characters

Table of Contents

Chapter 1: Unicorn Dreams

"I hold who I am in my heart, just like my Papi used to say."

— DAISY STARSHINE

Daisy was so excited she couldn't stop prancing, which is *not* what little donkeys usually do. Any minute now, her best friend, Clarissa, and her father, Mr. DeSilva, would arrive at the barn to bring Daisy her new brace. Then she'd *really* be able to prance.

Why is it taking them so long? Daisy worried. Maybe Mr. DeSilva couldn't make the brace. Or maybe he decided it wouldn't work after all. Fearing the worst, Daisy's prance turned into a slow circling in her stall.

To calm herself, Daisy thought of other things that her young friend Clarissa had made to surprise her. Daisy's favorite was her beautiful unicorn horn. A unicorn horn for a tiny donkey like her with one front leg shorter than the other was unusual, but it embodied what Daisy and Clarissa often dreamed about. They both loved unicorns and they both had issues with walking.

Since they first met, they had become inseparable friends. As a yearling in her homeland of Yucatán, Mexico, Daisy had become separated from her family during a torrential rainstorm. At that time, Clarissa and her parents were vacationing in Yucatán from their home in Southern California. Through a twist of fate, they ended up rescuing Daisy and taking her home with them to the United States. Clarissa's gentle brown eyes had immediately captivated young Daisy, and it didn't take long for Daisy to feel comfortable in her new home north of the border. Because of their close friendship, it was fitting that they would work together to master their similar physical challenges.

Daisy remembered the afternoon she received her handmade unicorn horn from Clarissa. Clarissa often brought a bag of toy unicorns into the barn to play with through the mornings and long afternoons. Daisy was both fascinated and envious of those toys. At times she felt left out because of how much attention Clarissa gave them. Daisy watched as Clarissa made the unicorns fly, do loop-de-loops, and move gracefully across the barn floor.

If only I could prance and fly like a unicorn, Daisy often sighed to herself. *Just walking without stumbling would feel wonderful. Unicorns are so magnificent, and I'm just a plain, little donkey.*

One day, as if she had read Daisy's mind, Clarissa said, "I wish *I* could be a unicorn, don't you?"

Daisy nodded and brayed excitedly, making a loud, nasal noise, which made Clarissa laugh.

Then Clarissa added sadly, "But you and I have to accept how we are. Both of us are little and have trouble walking." Clarissa sat down and folded her legs up underneath her. She fluffed her skirt to conceal the leg braces she wore.

Clarissa wore braces on *both* her legs and understood Daisy's feelings. But Daisy couldn't help wondering if being a little donkey with one leg shorter than the others was good enough compared to those whose legs were all the same length.

Clarissa startled Daisy when she abruptly jumped up and left the barn to go have lunch. She yelled back to Daisy, "I'm going to make you a present, and I'll bring it to the barn after I've finished."

Clarissa often surprised her, but Daisy couldn't imagine what this surprise could be.

Late that afternoon when Clarissa came back to the barn with her bag of toy unicorns, she also brought something else. She held up a long tube that came to a twisting point at one end. It was wrapped with shiny silver material and was sprinkled with colorful glitter.

"A unicorn horn!" Clarissa announced, her eyes sparkling.

Daisy brayed excitedly and pawed the ground.

Clarissa laughed and attached the horn to Daisy's forehead with a silver ribbon. It fit perfectly. Then she led Daisy to the drinking trough so she could admire her reflection in that watery mirror.

From that day on, Clarissa included Daisy in her play with the toy unicorns. And from that day on, Daisy was seldom without her horn. Somehow, when wearing it, she always felt better about herself.

The time had flown by as Daisy daydreamed about the time she received the graceful unicorn horn. Suddenly she heard the back door to the farmhouse crack open, and then the creak of the screen door. She heard the usual cough and spit from Clarissa's father, Mr. DeSilva.

"Eewww! Gross!" Clarissa said, giggling. Then came a higher-pitched throat-clearing and a dainty "petueee!"

"Good morning, Clarissa!" Daisy brayed loudly.

"It's not mmm-morning yet, little one," mooed a deep voice. That was Maribel, Daisy's friend. The old milk cow continued drowsily, "You're going to get the chickens squawking with that racket. Then old Reginald will start to … "

"Er-er-er, er-errrrr!" crowed Reginald, the rooster, before Maribel could finish complaining. The racket of chickens screeching and clucking filled the barn. Then came the sounds as they scurried around their pen, pecking the ground for the fresh meal Clarissa threw down.

"See what I mmm-mean?"

"Sorry, ma'am," Daisy apologized and scrambled to her feet with a little stumble. "I'm just excited. Today's the day I get to go to my new job at the racetrack where I'll be pulling the cleanup cart!"

"You didn't think I would forget, did you?" asked Maribel.

"No, ma'am," Daisy nickered. She began to dance around and stumbled again, but caught herself before taking a sudden spill.

"Careful now," Maribel laughed. "You don't want to hurt yourself, especially not today when you start your job at the horse track." Maribel pawed at a small pile of hay in the corner of her stall. "I've been working on something special for you all week," she said. With her teeth, she picked out of the pile a braided grass necklace. It had tiny flowers stuck securely into small knots along its length. The flowers had a yellow center surrounded by delicate white petals, connected to a bright green stem.

"Oh, Maribel! It's beautiful!" Daisy exclaimed. She limped over to her friend and raised her head so Maribel could place the flower necklace around her neck. Daisy moved to the water trough and beamed at her reflection.

"Braiding and tying those little knots wasn't easy," Maribel laughed.

"Thank you, ma'am. I love the daisies. Are *they* how I got my name?"

"Perhaps. Like a daisy, you *too* are beautiful and delicate," mooed Maribel. "But, child, looks don't reflect the truth or fullness of who someone is … neither does size or whether they stumble when they walk."

"I know," Daisy answered, as she looked down at the leg that almost made her take a tumble. "I hold who I am in my *heart,* just like my papi used to say in Mexico. But I'm not so sure about *this.* " She extended her right front leg, which was an inch shorter than her other legs. "Even if this doesn't stop me from doing my job pulling the cleanup cart, I'm afraid that the horses at the race track will make fun of me. After all, I'm just a little donkey, and they're all big racing stars."

"Child," Maribel soothed, "have you forgotten your last name is *Starshine*? Your *heart* is full of stars. They'll come out and shine when they're ready."

Maribel's words often reminded Daisy of the wise things her father used to teach her when she and her donkey family were together. And the love Maribel showed her was like that of her own mother back in Mexico. She missed her parents and her brothers, but that time felt long ago. Still, Clarissa had told her she overheard her own father and mother talking about taking Daisy to Mexico some day to help her find her donkey family. Although Daisy was excited about the idea, she believed that finding her family would be very difficult. Mexico was such a big place. For now Daisy decided to do one of the things her father had taught her. She put her worries aside, content with her peaceful life on the DeSilva farm.

As the early morning sunlight began streaming through the cracks in the old barn, the side door creaked open. Clarissa came in holding her father's hand. He held a bucket in his other hand and cradled a box under his arm.

Maribel mooed contentedly as Mr. DeSilva sat beside her on a stool and began the milking. As the first squirt of milk rang out in the tin bucket, Clarissa skipped over to Daisy, who nickered good morning. The little girl took the unicorn horn from the nail where she had hung it the night before and slipped it back onto Daisy.

"What a beautiful necklace," Clarissa said, fingering the delicate flowers draped around Daisy's neck. With a look of curiosity, she glanced at Maribel. She tilted her head in thought and then took Daisy's face in her hands and exclaimed, "I'm so excited! Today we train you to work at the horse track. I know you're a little thing like me, and you're probably worried about your leg. But Daddy always says, 'Don't let anybody say you can't do something just because you're small, or if you have a part of your body that doesn't work like the others. It's who you are on the *inside* that counts.' Look at *me,*" she added, doing a wobbly ballet turn on one foot that she called a *pirouette*. "I'm tiny like you, and I have braces on my legs, but I don't let it stop me. Besides, don't forget that I've got another surprise for you. Remember that Daddy made a brace for *your* leg too. It will help you walk better."

Daisy knew she was little. She stood only three feet tall at her withers, the ridge between her shoulder bones. Maribel warned her that the horses were known to be proud of their size and refined features. Maribel also warned her that they might poke fun at her tiny form and the fact that she walked with a limp. Daisy wondered if the brace Mr. DeSilva made for her would help.

"Well, it doesn't matter because I'm still growing," Daisy said cheerfully to Maribel. "And when I saw my reflection in the water, I noticed a pretty patch of white hair. It looked like a flower, maybe a daisy, growing on my forehead."

"I think it looks like a shining star," Maribel mooed after her.

Daisy giggled. "My papi had a shining star on *his* forehead. That's where my last name Starshine comes from. I like that even better!"

Clarissa clicked her tongue and Daisy followed her over to a stool. Mr. DeSilva, who had finished milking, sat back on the stool in front of Daisy. He reached into the box he had brought and removed an interesting leather device. It had a small boot at one end and two leather wraps above it. He tapped behind Daisy's shorter leg, and she lifted it. Mr. DeSilva slipped the boot over her hoof and secured the wraps with leather straps and buckles that fastened snuggly around both her lower and upper leg. When Mr. DeSilva put her hoof down, Daisy was amazed. All her legs seemed to be the same length now. She felt perfectly balanced!

"Okay, girl, try it out," he said kindly.

As Clarissa began walking away from her father, she turned and clicked her tongue, encouraging Daisy to follow her.

Daisy took one uncertain step, then another. She couldn't quite feel the dry straw or the wooden floor through the leather the way her *other* hooves did, but the brace felt fine. More importantly she was able to walk straight without a limp or a stumble.

Daisy brayed excitedly, while Maribel mooed encouragement. "Look at me!" Daisy cried.

"Good luck, child!" mooed Maribel as Clarissa led Daisy out of the barn into the bright sunlight.

They walked carefully through the chickens, who clucked worriedly, scattering in all directions with feathers flying. They made their way over to a covered horse trailer. Daisy could hardly keep from prancing with joy over her newfound mobility. Clarissa unlatched the doors of the trailer and pulled a metal ramp out from underneath. She lowered it at an angle to the ground and nodded at it. Daisy hesitated, then took two nervous steps back.

"It's okay, girl," Clarissa soothed.

Daisy had never seen a ramp or a horse trailer before and felt uncomfortable about them. Plus, she was just getting used to her brace. She wanted to think about this for a bit.

"Come on, up you go," encouraged Clarissa.

But Daisy wasn't ready. She didn't move.

Clarissa tried to coax her up the ramp with some crunchy oats. When that didn't work, she gently placed her hands on her rump and pushed. Daisy dug her hooves into the ground and leaned back. "Umph!" Clarissa exclaimed as she pushed harder, but Daisy wouldn't budge.

"You are being a naughty donkey," Clarissa scolded, then laughed and patted Daisy's head. "Daddy told me donkeys could be stubborn. I guess he was right. Look, I'll go up the ramp and into the trailer first to show you it's safe." She moved around Daisy and stepped backward up the ramp until she was in the trailer. "See, girl? Nothing to it. Now it's your turn."

Daisy took a breath and exhaled through her nostrils. She placed one hoof onto the ramp, then the other, which caused a metallic squeak. She waited for a second, then took a few more cautious steps. She hesitated at the darkness of the trailer. Then she smelled fresh oats and hay waiting for her inside. Because she was hungry, she clip-clopped the rest of the way in.

"Good girl!" Clarissa congratulated her and brushed her withers and back while she ate. Clarissa placed a halter on Daisy's head, pulling the straps up and over her nose and behind her ears. As she fastened the halter with a rope to the front wall of the trailer, she explained, "This will keep you safe and comfortable for the drive." Then she slid back a metal cover from a window by Daisy in the trailer, so she could look out.

"That feels much better," Daisy whinnied happily.

Chapter 2: A Special Friendship

Clarissa

"Your heart is full of stars. They'll come out and shine when they're ready."

—MARIBEL

"Oh, she's not just a donkey," Clarissa cheerfully corrected them. "She's my very best friend."

— CLARISSA

larissa and her father got into the truck that would pull the trailer. The engine coughed and sputtered to life, and Daisy caught her balance as the trailer lurched forward. She watched out the window as they drove down the long gravel drive and headed up the highway into the green hills.

Before long, Daisy saw the blue of the ocean through the swaying trees that lined the road. Daisy remembered the ocean. Clarissa had told her all about it. She even took her there once, shortly after finding her in Mexico and bringing her home.

Daisy remembered that day at the ocean when she was still a baby donkey, and Clarissa wore a bathing suit with a towel around her waist. Sitting in the truck, she held Daisy in her lap, with the little donkey wrapped in a colorful patchwork blanket that Clarissa's mother had made. When they arrived at the sea, Clarissa carried Daisy to the beach and set her down in the sand. It felt so warm, but the soft sand was hard for her to walk in, so Clarissa picked her up again and carried her toward a whooshing sound that was frightening and yet soothing to Daisy. Clarissa pointed and said, "There. Look at that, Daisy."

Daisy gasped. "Oh, my," she brayed, "is that the ocean? It's so big!"

Clarissa put Daisy down again, but this time the sand was wet, cool, and firm. It felt good beneath her hooves. The two of them ran back and forth along the shore and a bit into the water. Daisy ran with a limp beside Clarissa, who despite her braces managed to keep her balance. When a wave came, they turned and raced back to safety, laughing until they had to lie down and rest.

"We'll always be friends," Clarissa said softly as she toweled them off. Daisy felt so happy.

Today felt like that day, Daisy decided. Except the feeling was in her *heart* back then. It had felt warm and comfortable—secure. Today, the feeling was in her *stomach*. It felt like butterflies had found their way into her tummy and were fluttering about. Daisy decided this was what being excited felt like. She smiled and tilted her unicorn horn into the air.

Daisy watched out the trailer window as the truck cruised for miles over rolling hills and through valleys. They drove past groves of avocado trees, then sweet-smelling orange orchards, and a sparkling blue lake. The truck slowed and turned off the highway onto a winding dirt road. As the truck rumbled and bumped along, Daisy saw a cloud of dust billowing up into the air behind them.

Then, on the greenest grass she had ever seen, she thought she saw horses running. Before she could be sure, a fence blocked her view and then a tall, wide structure. Finally, they stopped at a tunnel-like opening where Daisy could see a reddish-brown track. Yes, there they were. The horses were far off and looked as tiny as Clarissa's toy unicorns.

Even from a distance, the horses took Daisy's breath away. "They're magnificent!" she brayed excitedly. "I can't wait to meet them." Just then the trailer lurched forward again and moved around the track. It stopped at a long wooden stable that had at each end large sliding double doors opened wide from their center. Most of the horse stalls on the exterior of the building had the top half of their Dutch doors open. A few of the stall doors were completely open. Light filtered into the stable and through the stalls to the interior space. The building and doors looked freshly painted. The names of the horses stood out in bold letters over each stall door.

They had arrived at the racetrack stable.

The first name Daisy read was "Jezebel." She pictured a gorgeous mare with a flowing mane. The next name was difficult to read, so she sounded it out slowly, "Ab-dul-Az-iz." She whinnied at the exotic sound of it. Finally, she read the next name, "Bull-Arch." "Oh my, that sounds powerful!" she exclaimed.

Everything was lovely, especially in comparison to the old barn where she had been living. Not that she was complaining. Although it was un-painted and had lots of cracks in the walls, Clarissa's family's barn was warm and comfortable. But *this* was magnificent. Everything was neat and in place. Even the gravel road had been raked, and the grass and bushes looked perfectly trimmed. The truck finally came to another stop when they turned the corner at the far end of the building. It parked in front of one set of the wide-open sliding double doors.

Clarissa climbed into the trailer and unfastened the rope that held Daisy in place. Leaving the halter on, she gently coaxed Daisy out and down the ramp, and then clicked her tongue.

"Come with me, girl. I'll show you your new home."

The idea of staying at this new place hadn't sunk in until now. Having endured the separation from her donkey family two years earlier, Daisy felt uneasy and confused. She suddenly missed her barn friends, Maribel and Reginald, and she stopped in her tracks.

"Oh my, are you going to be stubborn again?" Clarissa gently scolded.

Daisy nickered nervously, and Clarissa rubbed her ears, which helped to calm her down. Daisy took a breath and blew it out her nose. Then she followed Clarissa through the giant doors into the big interior of the stable.

They stopped at the first stall on the left. It had her name painted in bright pink letters over the door. "This one's yours, Daisy. Every day, you'll be the first one *out* and the last one *back*. Kind of like being in charge."

Daisy was amazed. The floor was spotless, the hay fresh, and the water cool and sweet. Clarissa reached into a pouch hanging over her shoulder and pulled out three framed pictures. The first was a picture of Daisy, and Clarissa hung it right over the place where she would sleep. The next was of Daisy's cow friend Maribel. That picture she hung a few feet away.

ust like her friend had been back at the barn. The last picture was of Reginald the rooster, and Clarissa hung that one in the opposite corner. Daisy began to feel a little more secure. Then Clarissa took out one more picture. She hung this one directly across from where Daisy would sleep. It was a picture of Clarissa. Now Daisy felt more at home.

"We'll start working tomorrow," Clarissa said. "First we'll get you used to your brace and then pulling the muck cart. That's what my daddy calls it. But I call it the cleanup cart."

Daisy had no idea what a muck cart or a cleanup cart was, but knew she'd find out soon enough. After munching some crunchy hay and grain, she followed Clarissa out into the sunshine. As they walked around the stable grounds, Daisy noticed men and women working around the place. Some were fussing with the plants or working on equipment. Others were cleaning and painting parts of the building, even though it was already so splendid.

Many of the people smiled as they passed and said a friendly "Good morning" to Clarissa. Several of them said, "What a fine-looking little donkey you have."

"Oh, she's not just a donkey," Clarissa cheerfully corrected each of them. "She's my very best friend."

That made Daisy feel so good that she lifted her chin high as she pranced ahead.

Chapter 3: Unkindness

As Daisy watched the huge horse, she sighed to herself,
"Magnificent."

—DAISY STARSHINE

"You should know you can't judge a book by its cover."

— CLARISSA

After passing some of the workers, Daisy heard a woman say, "My, she's such a tiny little thing." Another woman added, "I doubt she'll be able to pull the cart. And did you see that silly horn she's wearing?" Then she heard both women giggle.

A man who was painting a fence post stopped and watched them go by. Then he said to the women, "Not with that leg she won't." He snarled, "First it's DeSilva, always telling us how to do our jobs. Then his snippy little daughter comes along. Now this, a puny runt of a donkey who pretends to be a unicorn! And with a bum leg at that." He spit in the dirt and shook his head. He returned to his work, grumbling, *"I* should have been promoted to head groundskeeper, not him."

Daisy's feelings were crushed. She hung her head and felt discomfort from her brace. She wore the unicorn horn so often, she had forgotten it was still on. She wished she wasn't wearing it now.

Clarissa stopped abruptly, turned on her heel, and faced the workers. In a firm voice, she said, "Daisy can do anything she puts her mind to. She only got that brace this morning, and already she's walking as if she's worn it her whole life. As for the unicorn horn, I *made* that for my friend who is more special to me than you will ever know. She'll pull the cart better than anyone's ever done before. You'll see." Then she whispered loudly into Daisy's ear, "Don't mind Mr. Richardson. He's just a grump. Daddy says Mr. Richardson might have had a chance at promotion if he

16

wasn't so lazy and mean." Then she swung around and patted Daisy on her forehead. "Come, Daisy, let me show you around some places that are much prettier than this."

Daisy's spirits soared as she trotted happily away beside her friend. She was pleased that Clarissa was every bit as bold as the day they met. She thought she heard a couple of muffled "harrumphs" coming from behind them, and Daisy snickered at that. But then she heard the man say something under his breath. She knew she shouldn't pay him any attention. Still she twitched her ears to see if she could hear his comments.

"It's time I do something about this place. I'll show them. They'll be sorry they didn't promote *me* instead of DeSilva."

"There it is, Daisy," Clarissa's cheerful voice broke in. "That's the cart I was telling you about." She pointed to what looked like a wooden box on wheels.

Unlike everything else she'd seen so far, the cart was unpainted. It looked old and tired. The wood was dry, cracked, and stained as if it had seen its day of hard work. Daisy looked at the cart skeptically and dug in her heels. But it wasn't just the cart that was bothering her. She didn't like what she had heard the man say and she didn't know how to let Clarissa know. Whenever she felt unsure or uncomfortable, she did what donkeys tend to do and she became stubborn.

"Aw, don't be like that," Clarissa said. "You should know you can't judge a book by its cover."

Daisy stepped closer, hoping Clarissa was right. She saw an old rake and something that looked like a scoop on the end of a broom handle lying in the bed of the cart. Both looked as old and worn as the cart.

"I'll hook you up, and let's see how you do pulling it. It might be a little heavy at first, but I know you can do it." Clarissa reached into the cart and pulled out an old-looking harness that was rolled up inside. "Let's slip this over your shoulders and give it a try."

When Clarissa clicked her tongue, Daisy tried to take a step. The harness pulled tightly against Daisy's shoulders—but the cart didn't budge. Then Clarissa walked around in front of her and said, "Come on, girl; you can do it. Just lean forward a little more."

That did the trick. The cart creaked and squeaked as the wheels began turning. Daisy leaned into the harness and pulled the cart forward a couple of steps. At first it felt heavy, but once she got it moving, it wasn't so bad.

Clarissa laughed, saying, "I had better ask my daddy to oil this thing!" Stroking Daisy's nose, Clarissa added, "I also think it could use a fresh coat of paint. If we get started soon enough, we can have it all ready for opening day. Let's take it back to the stable and I'll get my daddy."

On their way, Daisy allowed herself to fantasize once more about being a unicorn. In her mind the old wooden cart became a grand carriage drawn by unicorns, and she was the leader. She pranced across the colorful land, her head held high, and guided the carriage toward a beautiful castle. Just as Daisy was about to draw the carriage into the air, her unicorn daydream was interrupted when she heard a horse's whinny and noticed three of the horses coming from the direction of the racetrack. They too appeared to be heading for the stable.

"Whoa, look girl," Clarissa said as she pulled Daisy to a stop and pointed toward the horses. "Aren't they magnificent?"

Daisy caught her breath, and her heart skipped a beat. She was amazed at the size and splendor of the horses. They seemed to glide effortlessly across the lawn toward Clarissa and her. To Daisy, it looked as though they were floating in the air just like the unicorns in her dreams.

"The one in front," Clarissa explained, "is Abdul-Aziz. He's an Arabian stallion. Look how he prances. He is high-spirited and very smart. His breed is one of the oldest in the world and used to be used in war. Arabians can run long distances and for long times, so he's especially good in endurance races."

Daisy looked at the stallion and whinnied to herself. *He must be five feet tall at his shoulders, and I bet he weighs eight hundred pounds.* His color was gray and his shimmering coat resembled a beautiful shade of brushed silver. The combination of sun and shadow emphasized his finely chiseled bone structure. Daisy's gaze trailed over his gracefully arched neck and his curved tail. He carried his tail high in the air, announcing confidence and pride.

Next, she saw a horse whose appearance suggested tremendous strength. This one was even taller than Abdul-Aziz. She had large, powerful muscles that bulged and rippled across her rich reddish-brown chest and hindquarters. The big horse suddenly shook her head, and her thick mane streamed into the air before settling back along her strong neck.

Daisy pawed the ground nervously.

"It's okay, girl," Clarissa assured her, patting her withers. "Jezebel is good at short races. Daddy says the races are only a quarter mile long, so horses like her are called Quarter Horses. Her breed originally comes from Spain. Cowboys are fond of horses like her because of their ability to make sharp turns and handle cattle. When she's not running quarter milers, she does barrel races. The barrels are kind of like cows," she laughed, "and she runs around them fast."

Daisy thought she couldn't feel any smaller or less significant. Then the third horse returning to the stable came into view. The first two had taken her breath away, but this one was *majestic.* Daisy sighed as she watched the huge horse.

"That's Bull-Arch," Clarissa said. "He's a Thoroughbred stallion." The awe in her voice was unmistakable.

Daisy couldn't believe horses could be that big, but he stood a full head taller than the others. Bull-Arch was the color of blackest coal, from his nose to the tip of his tail. Every rippling inch reflected the brilliant sunlight as he strutted across the grass.

"He's famous," Clarissa said. "He was named after two of the most famous Thoroughbred horses. One of them, Bulle Rock, was the first Thoroughbred horse brought to America. The other one was Sir Archy; he was so good at racing, he was eventually retired because no other horses could challenge him. My daddy says Bull-Arch might even be faster than him."

Bull-Arch approached with a walk that was more of a prance, suggesting great agility and athleticism. He shook his head and snorted, displaying his spirit and hot-blooded personality.

Aziz and Jezebel stopped just short of Daisy and Clarissa. Jezebel whinnied, "My, my, look at these pretty little ladies."

Daisy blushed and timidly pawed the ground.

"Aren't you just the tiniest little … *thing*?" Jezebel continued with a "we're better and more important than you" tone.

"Little?" Aziz joined in. "Puny, I'd say. How in the world is she ever going to pull that cart?"

Daisy felt the sting of their unkind words and cleared her throat, which embarrassingly came out sounding like "hee-haw." She remembered how her father had encouraged her about things like this in the past. She shook off her hurt feelings. She took a breath, then looked up into the faces of the two race horses and said curtly, "I'm pulling it just fine, thank you." Then she snorted as she looked off to the side.

Looking back at the horses' faces, she saw that their eyes had gotten big. Daisy felt pleased with herself that maybe her boldness had rattled them a little. She closed her eyes and shook her head at a bothersome fly. Suddenly it appeared that something had blocked out the sun. A shadow darkened the ground around her and when she looked up again, she saw the chiseled features of the towering Bull-Arch.

"What's the hold-up?" he snorted. Then, spotting Daisy, he asked, "What do we have here?"

"Exactly what we were wondering, Bull. What is it? A *unicorn?*" Aziz mocked in return.

"Looks more like a donkey-corn if you ask me." Jezebel laughed, shaking her flowing mane.

"Let me see ... " Bull said, as he sized up Daisy. "It's short and stubby, and its coat is dull and dirty grayish-brown." He tilted his head with a start. "I think it's a burro."

"And would you look at that," Jezebel chimed in. "Just what is that *thing* you're wearing on your leg? Is that a brace? Why, the two of you could be twins!" She snorted and stifled another laugh as she looked from Daisy to Clarissa and back again.

The sun reflected off Clarissa's shiny braces as Jezebel taunted them.

"All in all, I'd say it's even a little wider than it is tall!" Aziz exclaimed. He and Jezebel couldn't contain themselves and both burst into fits of whinnying.

Bull brushed the other horses aside and lowered his head to just above Daisy's. Then he asked her, "What are you doing here, kid?"

Daisy suspected he already knew. She felt flustered. She thought Bull was only looking for a reason to make fun of her. Even so, she straightened up and held her head with as much confidence as she could and answered. "Clarissa's father is the groundskeeper for the track, and our job is to keep it clean." Then she cleared her throat and said, "And, for your information, I'm a donkey."

"Do you mean the two of you are here to clean up the garbage?" Jezebel snorted with disgust.

"More like they're the poop patrol!" cracked up Aziz, and he and Jezebel erupted into a fresh burst of laughter.

"Well, I suppose *someone's* got to do it," said Bull. "But I had hoped for someone strong and capable and who wouldn't be an embarrassment to the track. Not a couple of crippled little things."

Clarissa couldn't understand what all the neighing, braying, and stomping of hooves was about. But she knew Daisy well enough to see that she wasn't comfortable. "Come on, girl, let's make this old cart look beautiful."

"Yes, *little* girl, get along now," Aziz mimicked Clarissa.

"Make that cart real pretty now, you hear?" scoffed Jezebel. "Maybe you could add some sparkles to it to match your pretend unicorn horn."

"Either way, I guarantee you'll be followed by lots of flies!" Aziz teased, and he and Jezebel snorted and laughed till their eyes filled with tears.

"You'll see, we'll do a great job!" Daisy said over her shoulder as she pulled the tired, squeaking cart away. At first, she sadly lowered her head and almost dragged her unicorn horn in the dirt. Then she tried to walk as properly as she could, although the harness was burning against her shoulders and her hoof was uncomfortable because she was still getting used to her brace.

"Just be sure you stay out of our way, runt," she heard Bull huff.

Chapter 4: Iridescent Puffballs

*Daisy remembered that her Papi would encourage her to
think about things that cheered her if she was frightened or
sad.*

When they got back to the stable, Daisy saw that Clarissa's father and a few other men had built a fence that extended out from the stable wall. As some of them used hay hooks to stack bales of hay, others used pitchforks to spread loose hay over the ground.

"Daddy, is it almost ready? Will they be here soon?" Clarissa asked excitedly. Then she clasped her hands over her mouth.

Daisy thought Clarissa looked like someone who had just given away a big secret.

"Should be ready in the morning, darling," Mr. DeSilva answered. He bent over, grunted from the effort, and picked up a heavy bale of hay. He carried it over and placed it next to a small stack of them.

It had gotten late, and Daisy hadn't realized how hungry she was. The excitement of the morning, along with practicing pulling the cart and encountering the three horses in the afternoon, had taken priority over her appetite. She felt like she could eat a whole cart full of hay and a bucket of oats too.

It felt good to be back in her new stall surrounded by pictures of her friends. And she loved listening to Clarissa sing as she brushed the dust from the day off her coat.

"Oh, my, the harness has rubbed your shoulders too hard," Clarissa said. She went over to a shelf where she took down a jar and opened it.

She stuck her fingers inside and took out a glob of rich, creamy ointment. She rubbed it into Daisy's hair. "This will help you feel better, and I'll have Daddy adjust the harness before you wear it tomorrow."

Daisy sighed as she felt the soothing warmth of the ointment on her sore muscles.

"Tomorrow, we'll paint the cart; then we'll start cleaning up around here. We'll even go out on the track," Clarissa added, patting Daisy's withers. "Sunday is opening day of the races. We'll make everything look nice. You'll see." Then Clarissa started humming as she tidied up the stable until her father called for her.

"See you bright and early," Clarissa smiled. "I'm bringing a surprise tomorrow. Sleep tight!" She kissed Daisy on the nose, hugging her close, and then left to join her father.

Daisy felt certain she could pull the cart now that she'd tried it. She was excited about beginning work and walking on the track for the first time. But she wasn't so sure the horses she met would be happy to see her. And they probably wouldn't appreciate her for the job she would do. The excitement she had felt earlier about moving to the racetrack was fading fast, now that she'd seen how mean the horses could be.

She lay down in the soft hay and tried to sleep. But her shoulders were still sore from the harness. Plus, worries about tomorrow kept popping into her thoughts. Like a swarm of bees, they spun around and around in her head. She looked at the pictures of her friends, hoping that might help calm her down. Instead, she found they only made her sad.

I miss my family and my friends, she thought. *If old Reginald was here, he would tell me a joke and make me laugh. And Maribel always helps me feel safe and loved.*

Daisy had plenty of soft hay to lie in. Still, she turned uncomfortably from side to side. Just when she found a good position for her aching shoulders, she thought she heard something. "Funny," she whispered, "it sounded like someone was trying to get my attention." She blinked once or twice, then decided it was just her imagination.

Settling down again, tears of loneliness welled up in her eyes. Daisy remembered that her father always encouraged her to think about things that cheered her if she was frightened or sad. She shook away the sadness and wondered what surprise Clarissa would bring tomorrow. Her thoughts drifted to the old stories Clarissa had told her about unicorns. In her mind she saw herself with a sparkling spiral horn in the middle of her forehead and with long slender legs. She also had feathered wings with which she could fly. She finally settled down and was just beginning to feel drowsy when she thought she heard something again.

"*Psst!*"

The sound was coming from above her. Pricking up her ears, she lifted her head and peered into the rafters. A few cobwebs caught the glow from the lights outside shining in through small cracks and holes in the stable wall.

"Oh, my," Daisy sighed. "I'm so tired and lonely. I must be imagining things."

Just then she felt the slightest tickle at the tip of her ear, and she wiggled it. Her ear tickled again, and this time she shook her head.

"Pssst!" she heard again, along with a tiny giggle.

"Don't tell me there are mice in here!" she snorted.

"Oh, heavens, no," a small voice answered.

Daisy brayed loudly and struggled to her feet with a start, swinging her head from side to side. Her eyes were open wide with fear as she tried to see who was there.

"*Whoa, whoa, whoa!*" the little voice called out. "Please don't be afraid!"

"Who are you? And *where* are you?" Daisy asked, her heart thumping wildly in her chest.

"I'm next to your right ear, silly."

Daisy slowly turned her head, but all she saw was the stable wall and Maribel's picture. She blinked hard, trying to get rid of the blurry, fuzzy thing near her right eye, but it wouldn't go away. Instead it moved slowly up and down and side to side. She blinked once more, but it was still there. Daisy wished she had fingers like Clarissa, so she could wipe it away.

The small voice said, "Step back. I think you might be too close to see me clearly."

"That's the silliest thing I've ever heard," Daisy retorted, despite her fear. "How can moving farther away help one see something more clearly? Maybe you should hold still." In a huff, she took a step back. Right before her eyes, the most exquisite creature she had ever seen slowly came into focus.

The creature was about the size of the tip of Clarissa's pinkie finger. It was round and very plump. It's color was black with shimmering bands of silver and brightly colored rainbow puffs of hair. She had heard Clarissa call that wonderful color *iridescent.* The creature was so fuzzy, it looked like a miniature cotton ball hovering in the air. Its wings whirred so quickly they were a blur.

"What are you?" Daisy asked, nervously pawing the floor.

"I'm a horsefly."

Daisy had seen flies before, but never one so big or beautiful.

"My name is Olivia," the creature added.

"You ... have a name?"

"Umm ... *yes!"* answered the fly.

"And you talk?"

"Don't *you?"* asked Olivia teasingly.

"I guess you're right. I'm sorry. My name is Daisy. I say silly things when I'm nervous."

"That's okay. Everybody does. I'm used to everyone screaming in horror and running away when they see me, crying 'Ahhhh! A fly!'" Olivia screeched, pretending to be afraid. To complete the effect, the horsefly bulged out her eyes as she raised her two front legs and waved them over her head. "I guess I *am* kind of big," she said, scratching her head with one of her side legs. "But how could I be that frightening? I'm just a horsefly, after all. I guess spiders can be kind of scary. I mean, *ew!*" Then she laughed, "But I wouldn't even hurt a fly."

Daisy chuckled at Olivia's antics.

"I hear you're the new cleanup crew," Olivia added. "Welcome to the stable."

"Yes," Daisy replied. "Tomorrow is my first day."

"So, why so sad?"

"I was excited about it at first, but now I'm feeling lonely. I miss my friends back home at our farm. How about you? Do you ever feel lonely in this big place?"

"Not at all. I'm surrounded by family and friends ... *and* the love of my life. Just look around," answered Olivia.

Daisy looked up. As she peered into the rafters she saw hundreds of tiny puffball-looking objects. They were silver, black, and iridescent and were hovering in the air just like Olivia. More horseflies. Other creatures were brown or black and were suspended by nearly invisible, silver threads. Each had brilliantly bright markings of orange, green, blue, or red that glowed in the dark, like lights. They looked like stars floating in the air. These were spiders.

Suddenly a bright yellow light blinked on just behind Olivia. A tiny fly half the size of Olivia appeared. He had black hair parted down the middle, a mustache that curled at the ends, and more hair growing from his chin called a goatee.

"Bonsoir, mademoiselle," the fly bowed and greeted Daisy in French.

"Everybody, this is Daisy," Olivia said.

All the little balls of fuzz waved and said, "Hello."

"Daisy, meet all of my friends. And last, but not least, is François."

"Hello, everyone," Daisy laughed. "I guess I'm not alone after all. But, Olivia, isn't François a firefly?"

"I beg your pardon, *mademoiselle,* I prefer *lightning bug,"* said François with a heavy French accent.

Olivia sighed and batted her eyes, murmuring, "Isn't he dreamy?" Then she refocused on Daisy. "We're all happy you're here, and I just know we'll be friends. Good night, kiddo!   See you around," she said, and buzzed gracefully up to rejoin the others. François spiraled away beside her, his tail light blinking on and off.

Daisy laughed as she swished her tail. Then she relaxed as she thought, *I don't feel so lonely anymore.* Soon she fell asleep and drifted into a peaceful dream.

★ ★ ★

Once again Daisy had transformed into a beautiful unicorn. Her coat was a sleek, shimmering white, and her mane and tail were streaked with the colors of the rainbow. Daisy skipped three times and lifted gracefully off the ground. With a single beat of her long, feathered wings, she soared above the stables and the race track. She could see the ocean in the distance. Daisy flapped her wings again and headed for home, her mane flowing behind her. Her heart lifted with happiness and excitement at the prospect of surprising her friends, and once more feeling safe and loved.

It didn't take long before she was able to see the old farm house, and behind that, the barn. Surprised to see that the area where Reginald and the chickens normally stayed was empty, she called out to announce her arrival.

This doesn't look right, she worried. *I should think I'd at least hear Reginald crowing by now.*

Daisy landed softly without ruffling a single feather, and noticed that the side door to the barn was open. "I bet they are all hiding inside to surprise me!" she nickered and folded her wings to enter. But inside the she saw no one, and heard only the clopping of her own hooves on the wooden floor.

"It's me, Daisy, I'm back!" she called, but heard only her echo in reply. "Here I am!" she brayed happily. But the barn appeared empty.

Finally, Daisy heard a noise coming from the back of the barn where it was dark. *That's where they're hiding,* she thought happily. *Pretty soon they'll all jump out and say surprise! But j*ust when she was about to enter the darkest part of the barn, she heard loud, shrill squeaking. She stopped, and a dozen or more shadowy creatures ran out of the darkness right at her.

"Rats!" Daisy shrieked and spread her wings to fly, but ceiling was too low. So she stood with all four of her hooves pulled in together, and hoped the rats would run past her. She trembled with fear. And just as the rats got so close their whiskers brushed against her legs, they split into two groups, and scurried around her. Daisy brayed in anguish for someone to help her, but no one did.

Just when she thought things could get no worse, she heard some curious laughter.

29

Chapter 5: Surrounded By Friends

DAISY - MARIBEL - REGINALD

"If you hope for things to ever change, you've got to start by loving and caring about yourself. Cheer your own self on. And every chance you get, no mm-matter how hard, give kindness to others. And you'll never run out of it. Because each time you give it away, mmm-more will grow inside you. That's how it works."

— MARIBEL

Daisy felt the warm sun on her face and she stirred. "Hey, little one. It's okay. It's only us," a gentle, familiar-sounding voice laughed. Daisy opened her eyes to the smiling face of her friend Maribel. Perched on the cow's back was Reginald, ruffling up his feathers preparing to crow. At first, Daisy thought she was still dreaming. Then she realized she was in the stable at the track, and morning sunlight was streaming into her stall.

"What are you two doing here?" Daisy nickered excitedly.

"Good mm-morning to you, too," Maribel laughed, and Reginald let go with a hearty "Er-er-er-er-err!"

"Surprise!" shouted Clarissa. She had just walked into the stable carrying a bucket and her bag of toy unicorns from home. She pulled up a stool, sat down, and clicked her tongue for Maribel to come for her morning milking. Reginald fluttered down, ruffled his feathers, and strutted toward the door of the stable.

"Leaving so soon?" Daisy brayed.

"My posse's out there, darling. I'm not one to keep the ladies waiting." With that, Reginald reached up with one wing, slicked back the brightly colored crest on his head, and strutted out.

"This is the surprise I told you about last night," Clarissa said between squirts of milk in the tin bucket while Maribel chewed her cud. "All of your friends will be living here with you from now on." Then she continued with rising excitement in her voice, "Daddy built an animal pen outside, and the track is going to have its first petting zoo! Maribel and Reginald will sleep in here with you because you three are the stars of the zoo."

Clarissa stood and wiped her hands on her jeans. "There, Maribel, all done for now. I'll take this milk to Daddy. When I get back, we'll go meet the others in the pen. Oh, yes, one more thing." Clarissa reached up and took Daisy's unicorn horn from the peg where it had hung overnight. "Can't be forgetting this," she said and fitted it to Daisy's head. Then with an "umph!" she picked up the heavy bucket and turned toward the door. Her leg braces softly clacked against each other and the milk made a splashing sound in the bucket as she walked away.

"Maribel, do you really think the people will be interested in a little donkey like me?" Daisy softly nickered. "A donkey with one short leg who pulls the poop cart?"

"Don't be silly. Everyone is going to love you. Besides, we're all together again. Let's be happy about that and mm-make the best of what we have. You don't see Clarissa letting her braces get her down, do you?"

"No, ma'am. You're right. It's just that yesterday I met some of the race horses and workers around here. They were pretty mean and made fun of Clarissa and me. I got so mad. I really wanted to tell them off."

"I'm so sorry. I know it feels bad when others are cruel," Maribel said gently. "But it won't help for you to hang your head, and it won't mmm-make things better if you return their mm-meanness. If you hope for things to change, you've got to start by loving and caring about yourself. Cheer your own self on. And every chance you get, no mm-matter how hard, give kindness to others. I know you've got plenty of that. And you'll never run out of it. Because each time you give it away, mmm-more will grow inside you. That's how kindness works."

Daisy was still amazed at how Maribel's wonderful sayings were so similar to her own father's wise teachings in Mexico. "Oh, Maribel, I'm so happy you're here," she brayed.

"That mm-makes two of us, child. I hear Clarissa coming."

Clarissa fastened the new brace onto Daisy's leg, and the three of them walked out into the large fenced enclosure. Sheep and goats meandered about. Ducks paddled contentedly in a large blue plastic pool in one corner of the pen. Reginald strutted in the middle of all the chickens. Daisy was surprised to see a few small goats. They seemed to like standing on top of the bales of hay. Daisy thought that if this was their attempt to feel bigger than they were, she could certainly understand.

As Daisy made her way around the enclosure meeting everyone, she noticed Clarissa on the other side of the fence. She was painting a cart that Daisy thought must be for the petting zoo. Clarissa called her over, opened the gate, and led her to the cart.

"I couldn't wait, so I took it home and painted it last night," Clarissa said. "I just put on some finishing touches. Daddy built a seat for me to ride on. He saw you pull the cart yesterday, and he said you're strong enough. What do you think?" Clarissa asked.

REFURBISHED CLEAN UP CART

Daisy couldn't believe her eyes. The cart was stunning. It was painted white, with bright red and blue trim. Even the scooper and the rake, which

34

Clarissa called a manure fork, looked clean, smooth, and varnished and hung neatly on the side of the cart. The old rusted caps at the center of the wheels were painted to resemble daisies. On both sides of the cart, painted in scrolling cursive letters, were the names *Clarissa & Daisy*. On the back end, in bold print, were the words *Track Cleanup Crew*. Even the harness looked fresh and clean. It was fitted with thick, fluffy pads that would sit right at Daisy's shoulders.

She couldn't wait to try it out, and she stood still, so that Clarissa could slip on the harness. Daisy wiggled her shoulders so that it would sit just right and she smiled happily. It was just as soft as it looked. Clarissa climbed up, sat on the bench seat, and took up the reins. She clicked her tongue and Daisy leaned into the harness. She was amazed. The cart moved almost effortlessly, and the wheels didn't squeak a bit.

"Daddy oiled something called the *bearings* in the wheels so they wouldn't squeak anymore, Daisy," Clarissa explained. "Isn't it wonderful?"

Daisy whinnied. She couldn't agree more as she pulled the cart with ease.

Every so often Clarissa reined the cart to a stop. Each time she hopped down and scooped up bits of trash or droppings left by the horses. Daisy noticed that although some of the workers waved as they went by, others turned up their noses. She was sure that some of them pointed at her unicorn horn and laughed at her. Some of them, including the mean Mr. Richardson from yesterday, even held their noses and wore looks of disgust.

"I don't know why some people get so upset," Clarissa mused out loud. "Horses have to poop … and someone has to clean it up." Then she giggled. "When I was little, I used to call their droppings *poo apples.*"

Daisy nickered at that.

There was a swarm of flies, friends of Olivia, trailing the cart. One of them flew right in front of Daisy's eyes. She could swear the fly had whiskers and a tiny piece of straw sticking out between his teeth.

"Howdy, ma'am," the fly said with a cowboy drawl. "The ladies on the prairie call them anything from *horse dumplings* to *cow patties* to *meadow muffins*. But I like to call them *buffalo chips.*" Then he buzzed away as quickly as he'd come.

Daisy laughed so hard, she snorted.

"You're doing a great job, kid," droned another fly, who was a big, husky fellow.

"I couldn't agree more," said a dainty-looking lady fly with a Southern accent.

"Thank you, ma-am," Daisy responded politely.

Clarissa pulled the reins in the direction of the stadium, and after a short walk through the tunnel they came to the edge of the racetrack.

Chapter 6: Horseflies

HORSEFLIES TO THE RESCUE

"Come on, fellas, lets snack on some hide!"

— TONY

*"Let us know if they give you any more trouble. We got
your back."*

— JEB

D aisy thought she had never seen such an attractive place. The dirt racetrack, a mile-and-a-half-long oval, was a deep reddish-brown. Inside this was a second track of lush forest-green grass. On one end of the interior track were two rectangular arenas. One was grass. Pairs of white wooden vertical posts were anchored into the ground with horizontal rails set between each pair at various heights. These fences were arranged in a seemingly random jumping course.

The other arena was dirt. It was equipped with three enormous metal barrels, positioned to form a triangle. Using the barrels, competitors had to finish a required pattern on the course.

The remainder of the interior section held a large, oval pond with a sparkling fountain. An assortment of single-level buildings that shone in the morning sun from fresh coats of paint completed the field.

A large door slid open in one building and out walked the three horses Daisy had met yesterday. Several others followed behind. Each horse had a person walking alongside, leading them with a long, sturdy rope. When they reached the center of the field, they separated and moved in three different directions.

Jezebel and a couple of other horses were led to the jumping arena. The woman leading Jezebel placed her boot into a stirrup and lifted herself up onto the Quarter Horse's back. Then off they went. Daisy watched,

38

amazed at the grace and agility with which Jezebel easily leapt over the rails as she made her way around the course. When she finished the jumps, she was led to the barrel racing arena. After several assistants changed the horse's saddles, Jezebel raced around the barrels at a dizzying speed. Daisy watched the other horses run the course. They did well, but Jezebel was clearly the fastest.

In the meantime, Aziz and Bull had been taken to the dirt track with the rest of the horses. Their handlers rode them counterclockwise around the large oval. Daisy watched with envy as these horses accelerated from a trot into a canter. She gasped in awe when they broke into a gallop. As they raced down the course kicking up dirt, their muscles rippled and their coats glistened with sweat.

She saw Aziz and Bull draw up alongside each other and wondered who would be the fastest. They ran neck and neck for several lengths of the track. Both of them easily pulled away from the pack of other horses. They eased around the far end of the track, still matching one another's pace. Then just after they came out of the curve, Bull rocketed away, taking the lead. Daisy's heart skipped with exhilaration and she pawed the ground with her braced leg.

The two horses foamed at the mouth as they headed toward the finish line where Daisy and Clarissa stood with the cart. The steeds thundered past them in a cloud of dust with strides so powerful Daisy felt the pounding of their hooves on the track. After crossing the finish line, the horses finally slowed and walked leisurely around the track to cool down.

"They're not even running all out yet, Daisy!" Clarissa yelled with excitement. "Wait till you see them on race day. You simply won't believe it!" Then she added, "It's our turn now," and she guided Daisy onto the track.

The reddish-brown dirt felt wonderful under her hooves as Daisy made her way around the track, pulling the cart. She had always dreamed of becoming a unicorn, but at this moment she closed her eyes and imagined herself a powerful, racing, *Thoroughbred* unicorn.

In her mind, Daisy heard the roar of the crowd as they cheered her and her competition on. Then she heard the labored breathing and pounding hooves of the other thoroughbreds. She was the underdog, but little did the crowd know, she had been holding herself back for the critical moment when she would break away and leave the others in her wake.

While rounding the first bend, she was behind the others. All she could see were the rear ends of the horses in front of her. And all she could taste was the dirt they kicked up into her face. But Daisy patiently savored the moment she was waiting for.

By the time the pack of horses began the final curve, Daisy had passed several of those lagging behind, and the volume of the cheering crowd increased. Finally, the group made it out of the curve and headed down the straightaway. This is where Daisy pulled out all the stops. She edged between the two front horses. Then she ducked her head, pushed her muscles to the max, and accelerated with every thing she had left.

Daisy's hooves left the ground as she blew past the lead horses as if they were standing still. She glided through the air with ease, her mane and tail flying out behind her. She was so far in front of the pack, she did a couple of loop-de-loops. Then with the crowd on their feet, waving hats in the air and chanting her name, she landed and focused on the finish line.

She saw each grain of rust-red sand before her. Her galloping front legs were sleek, slathered with sweat, and powerfully striding to the finish less than a furlong away. Daisy pounded the ground, and the distance lessened to half a furlong, then a quarter! She knew the finish line, the roses, news crews, flashing cameras, and flowing champagne were mere hoof beats away!

"Daisy? Daisy!" Suddenly Clarissa's voice broke into her fantasy. "Daisy! What are you doing?"

Daisy opened her eyes and realized she had reared up in her harness and was pawing at the air. She looked sheepishly at Clarissa and dropped down on all four hooves.

"Look, Daisy, they're coming to see us again."

"If it isn't the little pooper-scooper … and a unicorn, too! How cute," whinnied Aziz.

"Does she think she can actually run with us?" Jezebel sneered. "Take a look at yourself, tiny girl. Oh … *I* know," she laughed, "maybe with your special unicorn powers, *you* think you can fly."

Daisy lowered her head and glanced miserably up towards her unicorn horn. She suddenly felt like a fool.

Aziz raised his tail, and Daisy heard the plop, plop, plop. "You missed something," he nickered. "You should dump the load you have and come back for this. It might be more than you can carry with that leg of yours. You know, Bull, I think this job suits her. She blends in perfectly with all those flies."

Both Jezebel and Bull chuckled. Then Bull cleared his throat and said, "I told you to stay out of our way!" He reared up on his hind legs, shook

his head, and came down hard. Foam and sweat sprayed over Daisy and Clarissa, and the three trainers came running over. They draped the white lead ropes over the three horses' heads and began pulling them back. Before the trainers turned them, Bull growled, "Next time, I won't go so easy on you, kid. You don't belong here."

"Let's get out of here. These flies are disgusting," Jezebel said, wildly swishing her tail.

Just then the big, husky fly from earlier buzzed up to Daisy. "Excuse me, but it occurred to me that I haven't introduced myself. I'm Tony, at your service. I couldn't help but overhear the conversation here. If I'm not mistaken, these three horses aren't exactly friends of yours, are they?"

"You could tell, huh?" Daisy replied dejectedly.

"Hey!" the fly suddenly hollered at the horses. "Who are you fools saying is disgusting?"

The horses stopped and turned around, their ears flattened back in rage.

Tony turned to the cart. "Hey, boys and girls! Seems we got some business with the big, four-footed hairy things over there that call themselves … horses!"

For a moment there was silence as all the buzzing flies stopped their feeding frenzy.

"Hmm, kind of a coincidence, wouldn't you say?" Tony asked Daisy. "Me, Jeb, and the others here just so happen to be horseflies. Come on, everyone, let's snack on some hide! The boys will rough them up and keep them busy while the ladies sample their blood."

Hundreds of flies buzzed up around Tony. Jeb hollered, "Yeehaw!" and the whole mass of them flew straight for the horses.

Bull reared up, madly shaking his head. Aziz made a sound that could only have been a scream as he frantically shook his flanks. Jezebel's eyes bulged. The three of them twisted around, pulled free of their handlers, and galloped away, surrounded by a black cloud of angry horseflies.

"Well, I don't know what got into them," Clarissa said. Then she hopped down from the cart, grabbed the scoop and fork, and cleaned up the mess.

Daisy thought that if she had it her way, she'd just as soon fling every bit of the smelly manure at the race horses. Then she'd join the flies in showing them what's what. But Clarissa climbed back onto her seat and guided Daisy to the bin where she dumped the work of the day. Clarissa put on some long rubber gloves. Then she sprayed the bed of the cart with a hose and scrubbed it with soap and a long-handled brush until it looked and smelled as good as new.

By the time Clarissa finished, Tony and the rest of the swarm had returned.

"You didn't hurt them, did you?" Daisy asked.

"Nothing too serious, darling," he grinned. "But they're going to look kind of lumpy tomorrow from our horsefly-bites."

"Let us know if they give you any more trouble," Jeb drawled, chuckling. He picked

his teeth with the piece of straw. Then he spit in the dirt and said, "We have your back." Then he and the swarm flew away for the night.

Chapter 7: Fire!

FINDING YOUR STRENGTH

"The best criticism of the bad is the doing of the better."

—DAISY'S PAPI

*Daisy believed in her heart doing all she could do to
save them was the right thing to do.*

Daisy was glad the flies helped her, but as she tried to eat, her heart still sank in sadness. Listening to the cruelty from the race horses was exhausting and devastating.

"I have some good news for you, Daisy!" Clarissa said excitedly as she came into the stall. "Daddy said I can sleep in the stable tonight, and my mother agreed too. We'll all be together … you, Maribel, Reginald, and me!"

This news cheered up Daisy. But as she ate, she wished she could return to the safety of the DeSilva family barn. She wondered how long she could stand working at the track.

Putting these thoughts aside for now, Daisy focused on enjoying the sleepover with Clarissa and her other friends. Mrs. DeSilva set up a cozy cot for her daughter next to Daisy. She hung a lantern on the wall behind Clarissa's bed so she could read her storybooks. Tonight, she brought one of Daisy's favorites, which was full of pictures of elegant flying unicorns. Clarissa removed Daisy's leg brace and then her own braces. Maribel and Reginald drew close and listened to their friend read.

Maribel and Reginald gradually fell asleep, and it wasn't long before their peaceful snores filled the room. But Daisy and Clarissa sat up enjoying each other's company long into the night. Eventually Daisy noticed Clarissa's voice beginning to trail off. Then in the middle of a sentence, the book dropped out of Clarissa's hands, as she too fell asleep. Daisy nosed the book off Clarissa's tummy and pulled the blankets up to her friend's chin. Then she snuggled down into her hay for the night.

But as soon as Daisy felt her eyes flutter closed, a noise across the way startled them open again. She got up and walked softly to the interior door of her stall. She peered at a darkened window on the other side. At first there was silence, then the sound of a car door closing quietly. A light came on, illuminating the window, and through it she saw a door open to the workroom on the other side. Then she saw the yard man, Mr. Richardson, the one who had said those mean things about Daisy, Clarissa, and her father, come in through the door.

He was carrying two large cans in each of his hands, which he placed on top of a barrel. Daisy could barely make out the odd-looking symbol on the cans, but it looked like a human skull and crossbones. She didn't know what this meant, but it made her feel uncomfortable. Mr. Richardson stacked some boxes that blocked the cans from view, then nodded and walked back outside the stable.

Daisy sensed something was wrong but realized there was nothing she could do about it. She decided the best she could do was to pay special attention to that man. Then an idea came to her. "Olivia!" she called, and down from the rafters came the whirring iridescent ball of fuzz.

"What is it, Daisy?"

"I'm worried," Daisy said, and explained about the man she saw with the cans and the strange-looking symbols. "Will you ask François to go over there to see what's in those cans?"

François's light flashed on. "But of course, *mademoiselle*. I am at your service." He bowed, then fluttered across the stable to the workroom and disappeared among the barrels. All Daisy could see was a faint glow that followed him. Less than a minute later, he returned to Daisy's stall.

"Those are only gas cans, *mon amie*," he reported. "That man ees probably responsible for putting gas into some of the machines around here, like the lawn mowers; that ees all."

"I'm sure it's nothing," agreed Olivia.

"Hmm, maybe," Daisy said, "though it seems strange to do that kind of work in the middle of the night. Thanks for checking."

47

As her two friends returned to the rafters, Daisy wondered if perhaps Olivia could be right. She was worrying for nothing. Just the same, she decided to stick to her plan of keeping an eye on the man. But for now, she needed sleep. She walked in a small circle until she found the softest spot in the hay. Then she lay down and closed her tired eyes. Soon she was fast asleep.

"Wake up, Daisy! Something's wrong! Can you smell it?"

Daisy awoke with a start to Olivia's raised voice in her ear. Immediately she smelled the pungent odor of smoke. She looked over groggily to where Clarissa had been sleeping and saw that she wasn't in her bed anymore.

"Where's Clarissa?" she asked.

"She got up a while ago and went to her parents' trailer. What do you think that smell is?"

"I don't know, but I think it's coming from inside the stable."

At that moment, Daisy heard some coughing coming from the stalls of the race horses. She stuck her head out the small window in her stall door. She could see the heads of Aziz, Jezebel, and Bull sticking out of their stall windows. Their eyes bulged with fear.

"I don't see fire, but I sure smell smoke," she said with alarm, pulling her head back in. "Olivia, can you please send François to check?"

"On my way, *mon amie*," said François, whose lightning bug light came on at the mention of his name. He flew out the window, sniffed the air, then took off toward the far end of the darkened stable, on the other side of the horses' stalls.

In the time it took Daisy to wake Maribel and Reginald, François flew back in through the window shouting, *"Fire! Fire! And eet ees heading this way!"*

"What do we do?" asked Maribel.

"We've got to tell Mr. DeSilva," Daisy answered urgently. She pushed against the door to her stall, but it didn't budge. "We're locked in!" she said, looking nervously at her friends.

The coughing and whinnying of the horses had gotten louder. Daisy could hear them stomping fearfully on the wooden floor. She looked out the window again and saw flames climbing up the inside of the stable. Fire was popping and crackling, burning everything it touched. It belched clouds of irritating smoke as it raged toward the horses' stalls. She knew it would come to hers next. Then Daisy realized the fire could even put Clarissa in danger if it wasn't stopped.

"We've got to get out of here!" she cried and pushed against the door — but again it didn't budge. "Maribel, you try!" she shouted.

Maribel leaned into the door with all her weight, but it stayed closed tight.

Daisy knew Reginald was too small to be able to force the door open, and she realized Olivia and the others would not be able to alert Clarissa. She began to panic, and cried, "What can I do? I'm just a weak little donkey!"

"That's it!" Maribel shouted. "You're a donkey!"

"I know I'm a donkey. So what?"

Maribel turned to Daisy and asked, "What are donkeys known for?"

"Uh, we're stubborn?"

"Yes, but what else?"

Daisy snapped, "This is not a good time for riddles, Maribel! We have to find a way out!"

"What do donkeys do better than anyone else?" Maribel asked.

"Bray … loudly?" Daisy answered, shaking her head.

There is one thing you can do better than all of us. Even better than those horses! Think!"

Daisy was becoming frustrated with Maribel. In anger, she paced around the room, tripped over a five-gallon bucket of water, and reared back and kicked the container as hard as she could, sending it across the room and crashing into the far wall.

"That's it!" Maribel said triumphantly. "You're a donkey, and donkeys have powerful kicks!"

Daisy looked up at her friend, her eyes filling with tears. "You're right," she said, her voice full of wonder and sudden understanding. "I was born to kick. Move back everyone!"

Daisy walked back to the door and turned around. She kicked the door with her back legs, but nothing happened. She cleared her throat, took a deep breath, and kicked again, harder this time. But this still did nothing more than rattle the door on its hinges. She became spitting mad, leaned down with her front hooves, and kicked with everything she had — and boom! The door exploded open with a bang.

"Okay, Maribel," Daisy said, taking charge. "You wake Clarissa and her parents and get all the animals out of the petting zoo! Move out!"

"I'm mmm-moooving!" Maribel said and strode off briskly—as briskly as Maribel *could* move out the door.

"Reginald, you break the fire alarm glass with your beak! Olivia, you and all your friends get out of here and wait outside!"

"On our way. But what about you?"

"I'm going to get those horses out," Daisy answered with determination. She left her stall and turned toward the horses, but she saw that the fire had already separated her stall from theirs. She would burn up before she could get them out. Then she had an idea. She followed the spiders and flies out of the stable and through the petting zoo. Daisy was pleased to see the zoo animals had already been let out of the pen—probably by Maribel. As she turned the corner of the building, she saw Maribel bumping the door to Clarissa's family trailer. A light came on inside. Thank goodness, she thought, and ran around to the front of the stable. She heard the alarm bell ringing and knew Reginald had been successful at his assignment. She hoped she could do hers.

As Daisy approached the horse stalls from the other end of the stable, she heard them whinnying in terror and trampling the floor with their hooves. She couldn't understand why they hadn't kicked their own doors down but decided now was not the time for such questions. She knew that holding a grudge against these horses was what some would expect. But she decided if grudges were to be held, they would not be by *her*. As if it were yesterday, Daisy heard her father's voice in her head. *"The best criticism of the bad is the doing of the better,"* he used to say back home in Mexico. Daisy believed in her heart that doing all she could to save them was the right thing to do.

First Daisy went to Jezebel's stall, shouting, "Jezebel, get away from the door!" Daisy backed up against the door, leaned her nose to the ground, and with one powerful kick busted it right off its hinges. The door fell with a thud. Jezebel ran past Daisy out to the grass across from the stable where she promptly rolled on the ground to cool down and rid herself of the smell of smoke.

Next, Daisy yelled to Aziz to stand back. Aziz could be heard thrashing and stomping in terror, the fire licking at his stall. Daisy kicked down his door too. His eyes bulging and nostrils flaring, Aziz, too, galloped past Daisy and joined Jezebel on the grass.

Then Daisy came to Bull's stall. The fire was already in his stall. So, without hesitation, she blasted the door with her powerful back legs and rock-hard hooves, and it broke into pieces.

Bull left his stall in a statelier manner than either of his friends, even though the end of his tail was singed and smoking. He saw Daisy, panting and out of breath, and leaned his face down to her and rasped, *"We owe you our lives."* He looked like he was in shock as he joined the other two horses.

Daisy saw Mr. DeSilva and several track workers dragging large hoses across the ground. As the powerful water came gushing out of the hoses, they drenched the front of the stable and the horses' stalls. Smoke billowed into the air. Others dragged their hoses around the back to aim the forceful water into the other areas. Then Daisy saw Clarissa and, grateful she was safe, coughed out a puff of smoke and collapsed in an exhausted heap.

"Daisy! You saved them, you saved the stables and everything!" Clarissa cried as she hugged Daisy's neck. Moments later, Daisy heard sirens and soon saw the flashing lights of fire engines, ambulances, and police cars racing toward the stable.

Chapter 8: Cow Patties & Spiderwebs

MARIBEL

*"The guilty talk the loudest because they have something
to hide."*

— MR. DESILVA

The fire was put out quickly by the firefighters. It appeared most of the damage was to the back side and interior workroom of the building. Luckily it had barely touched the stalls.

Daisy heard people wondering out loud how the fire could have started, and she thought about Mr. Richardson. He was standing around with the rest of the workers and, louder than the others, was asking about the fire. Daisy remembered Mr. DeSilva once telling Clarissa that sometimes the guilty talk the loudest because they have something to hide.

As she wondered what she could do about it, Maribel came over to her. "I feel awful admitting this," she said, "but I think that mm-man stepped in one of my patties." She nodded in the direction of Mr. Richardson. "Just before bedtime, I took a walk around the building to do my business. And just a second ago, I was standing near him, and I swear I could smell it. Poor fellow has got it all over his boots. I think he slipped in it too from the looks of the back of his pants. That mm-man is going to be after mmm-me for that," she worried.

Mr. Richardson had turned around and, sure enough, Daisy could see the telltale signs that he had slipped in some manure. It was all over the seat of his pants, and the flies were swarming around him.

"I think we may have something here," Daisy said. She nudged Clarissa to her feet, then with her nose pushed her gently toward the back of the stable.

"What are you doing, Daisy?" Clarissa questioned. But Daisy persisted and eventually came upon several large cow droppings. She could see that someone had indeed slipped in one of them. Then she saw what she was looking for. Right in the centers of two other patties were boot imprints. She nudged Clarissa some more, hoping she would see what she saw.

"Would you look at that?" Clarissa finally said. "Those boot prints are awfully close to where this fire seems to have started. I wonder who they belong to?"

That was all Daisy needed. She promptly began nudging Clarissa back around to the front of the stable toward Mr. Richardson.

He was standing a few yards away from his truck and scowled when he saw them coming. He turned his back on them and swatted helplessly at the flies around his pants. Daisy could tell by the look in her eyes that Clarissa had spotted the smudge on the man's rear end. This was proof that he had recently slipped in a cow pie.

Daisy hadn't noticed until now that Olivia's spider friends had been holding on to her mane all this time. As they loosened their grips, she felt a thousand little tickles and then saw them leap into the air and land on Mr. Richardson's truck. At the same time, she saw François and Olivia fly over there, and François disappeared under a tarp in the bed of the truck.

François reappeared a moment later and signaled to Olivia who signaled to the spiders. The spiders began spinning a web that quickly covered the truck's cab door. Reginald had also flown over to the vehicle. Perched on top of the cab, he ruffled his feathers, lifted his beak to the sky, and loudly crowed. Reginald drew everyone's attention and silenced them all at once.

"What's this?" asked Clarissa, as she walked over to the back of the truck. She reached over and grabbed an end of the tarp.

"Leave that alone!" hollered Mr. Richardson. "That's private property!"

But as he uttered those words, Clarissa flicked the tarp in the air, revealing several gas cans underneath. She tossed them, one after the other, to the ground and said firmly, "How curious. They're all empty."

The crowd of people turned to look at Mr. Richardson as he headed straight for the truck's front door. When he tried to open it, he found it had been completely webbed over. He recoiled with a short, high-pitched scream.

"Ahhh! Blasted spiders!" he screamed. Then he turned and started around to the other door. But he ran smack into the back end of Maribel, who had quietly moved to just that spot, and there he fell down.

Mr. Richardson groaned, scrambled to his feet, and then bolted away as the crowd watched in shock. He ran past Daisy, who turned and with a properly placed kick to the man's backside, sent him staggering past Jezebel. She casually stuck out a foreleg, tripping the man to the ground with a thud.

Bull walked over and with his teeth picked the man up by the seat of his pants and carried him back to the truck. Then he dropped him in the dirt. The crowd gathered around him as Mr. Richardson sat in a heap, grumbling and trying to brush the dirt off himself. Everyone looked suspiciously back and forth between the spectacle of him and the empty gas cans.

"I'm not responsible! I've done nothing wrong!" he fumed. Then, blubbering almost incoherently, he continued, "What are you all looking at? You should be doing something about these animals. Can't you see they've all gone mad?"

"Daddy," Clarissa said, "Daisy and I found boot prints on the side of the stable where the fire was started. Have him show you his boots." But this was hardly necessary. Everyone could see the boots were still caked with manure.

"Officers," Mr. DeSilva said, "can you arrest him?"

"We can hold him until we get a good look at those boots. We'll check them against any prints we might find around the fire source. If they match, he'll be going away for a good while."

One of the police officers handed Mr. Richardson a bag. "Put those boots in here; I don't want them stinking up my vehicle. And wrap yourself in this clean blanket." Then he put him in his squad car and drove off to the station.

The fire crew finished mopping up and then headed back to the station along with the paramedics. The horse track veterinarians had arrived to check the health of the animals. It was still late at night, but the lights that lined the stable illuminated the area. All eyes were now on Daisy. She was trembling as she stood there, Clarissa's arms around her neck. Mr. DeSilva walked up to them.

"I don't know how you did this," he said to Daisy, "but you probably saved this place and all of us. You're a hero, Daisy."

Everyone encircled Daisy. They patted her head and withers, smiling and chanting her name. Daisy looked up, tears of relief in her eyes. She noticed that the three horses had gathered around her as well. She sighed, wondering what cruel words they might have for her now.

"I underestimated you, Daisy," said Bull sheepishly. "We all did. I'm very sorry."

"If it wasn't for you," Jezebel added, "we would no longer be such magnificent race horses. We'd all be nothing but crispy critters."

"We're not the stars here, Daisy," said Aziz. *"You* are."

The three horses bowed their heads and in unison said, *"Thank you."* Then Bull stepped closer, looking down awkwardly for a moment, and then straight into Daisy's eyes. He cleared his throat, and spoke softly.

"We owe you a huge apology, Daisy. We were just terrible to you this week, and you owed us nothing. And yet you still saved our lives. You've shown us that there is *never* an excuse for cruelty. You are someone of true honor and kindness, and we have learned from you what a *true* star is. It's someone who does the right thing, no matter what. *Thank you from the bottom of our hearts."*

Daisy could scarcely believe her ears as she listened to his words. The other horses nodded in agreement, and they all had tears in their eyes. Daisy replied with a catch in her throat, "You are *so* welcome ... all of you."

"Okay, everyone, it's been a wild night, and I know we're all excited," Mr. DeSilva said. "But there's still enough time till morning for us to get a little sleep before opening day. We have plenty of hay in the petting zoo for the horses to make their beds tonight. Let's get them in there and try to get some shut-eye. Tomorrow morning, we'll get up early to tidy things up."

As Daisy made her way back to her stall, she suddenly stumbled. She looked at Maribel, then at her right front leg. She realized for the first time tonight that she had done everything *without* her brace. In wonder, she looked at Maribel again.

Her friend mooed softly and winked at her. "See what you can do when you're not thinking about it?" she said.

Chapter 9: The Clouds Have Cleared

"I've heard that sometimes the brightest stars are never seen. Every once in a while, the clouds clear and your star gets to shine."

— BULL-ARCH

"I'm happy just the way I am!"

— DAISY STARSHINE

Daisy woke to see dust particles floating in the shafts of sunlight that penetrated the cracks and holes of the stable wall. The spiders were awake and mending their webs in hopes of catching breakfast.

"Morning, Daisy!" Clarissa sang out, skipping happily into the stall. "Let's get that brace on. We've got some work to do."

They left the stable together. Maribel and even Reginald were still asleep, which was most unusual. They went through the petting zoo where Aziz, Jezebel, and Bull were already being brushed in preparation for their races. Up and down the road in front of the stable they picked up bits of debris as birds sang and bees buzzed their morning songs. All the workers greeted Daisy and Clarissa with friendly "Hellos" and big smiles. Daisy happily thought how good it felt just to be alive on such a glorious day.

The morning moved along quickly and Clarissa hummed to herself as they worked. Then Daisy heard the clip-clop of horses. She turned and saw the three of them with their trainers. They were coming right toward her. She was anxious to find out if they would return to scorning her as they had before last night.

"Morning, Daisy!" Jezebel dipped her head and whinnied.

"Hey, champ!" called out Aziz.

"Well, if it isn't the star of the show!" greeted Bull sincerely.

"*You* three are the stars of the show! You're who everyone is coming to see, not me," responded Daisy as she brayed happily at their kind words. Then she lowered her voice. "To be honest, I'm feeling like this little star will always be hidden behind the clouds."

"Daisy," said Bull, who stopped in front of her. "I've heard that sometimes the brightest stars are never seen. But I think today will be different." He reared up on his hind legs and whinnied, "You're the brightest star of all!" When he came back down, he bent his head close to hers and winked. Then he turned and rejoined the others as they made their way to the track.

Daisy heard the roar of the crowd as it welcomed the spectacular race horses. Her heart was bursting with pride about saving the animals and the stable from the fire last night. She still felt astonished by the kindness of the horses and Bull's compliment. Still, Daisy wished there was some way she could take part in the races, even if it was only to watch. She consoled herself by reasoning that, after all, she was only a donkey—and a rather small one at that. But then, reasoning alone doesn't always help one feel better.

"Mmm-move over, friend."

Daisy turned and was surprised to see Maribel with Reginald sitting on her back. They were coming toward her and were led by Mr. DeSilva.

"What are you two doing out here?" Daisy asked.

"Oh, it's not just the two of us, child. We brought some friends along too," Maribel answered.

Daisy saw that what at first looked like a funny hairdo was really all of Olivia's spider friends from the barn on Maribel's head. They were riding between her ears and all of them were jumping up and down, waving at Daisy. Then she noticed Olivia, François, and the rest of the flies swarming over, and they hovered around her.

"Well, then, what are all of you doing out here?" she laughed.

"You'll see soon enough," Maribel said merrily.

"Ready, Clarissa?" Mr. DeSilva asked his daughter.

"Ready, Daddy ... Oh wait! I almost forgot." She reached behind her and took out the unicorn horn she had made for Daisy and tied it on her head. Daisy was surprised to see that Clarissa had freshened it up with new sparkles. "Okay, ready!"

"Let's go," said Mr. DeSilva, and Clarissa clicked her tongue for Daisy to move forward toward the tunnel to the racetrack.

When they emerged from the tunnel and onto the track, Daisy saw Jezebel, Abdul-Aziz, and Bull-Arch standing together like statues. The horses held their heads and tails at attention as though they were saluting her. Daisy felt confused. Clarissa reined her to a stop directly in front of them, then turned her to face the stands. Clarissa's father was handed a microphone and the entire place fell silent.

"Ladies and gentlemen!" Mr. DeSilva's voice called out through the loudspeakers. *"Welcome to opening day!"*

Daisy jumped a little when the crowd erupted in cheers and applause.

"We'll be getting underway in just a few minutes," Mr. DeSilva continued. "But first, let me explain why you're seeing this rather unusual gathering before you this morning. Here we have a donkey, my daughter Clarissa, a cow, and a rooster. And, although you probably can't see them, there are a lot of tiny spiders, horseflies, *and* a firefly."

He went on, "I'm sure you noticed the burned back side of the stable as you came in. Well, last night, someone tried to burn down our stable."

A loud gasp from the crowd filled the stadium. It was followed by a hush.

"It's okay, folks," Clarissa's father continued. "The fire was put out, and the person responsible was caught and arrested." He turned and raised his arm, motioning toward Daisy and the others. He said, "Because of their brave efforts, the stable and the lives of these incredible race horses … and who knows how many other lives … were saved! None of that would have been possible if it weren't for the quick, heroic action of one of them in particular … our dear donkey, Daisy!"

Daisy looked up suddenly at the mention of her name. She couldn't believe her ears. The horses and all her friends formed a large half circle around her. Then over the loudspeaker she heard Mr. DeSilva say, *"Daisy, please take a bow!"*

Tears filled Daisy's eyes as the people in the stands stood cheering. Her friends clapped, whinnied, mooed, crowed, and buzzed. *If only my family back in Mexico could see me now,* Daisy thought.

The crowd began to chant, *"Dai-sy! Dai-sy! Dai-sy!"* And the joy she felt last night came rushing back.

After Daisy bowed, Clarissa climbed back on the cart and directed her to walk around the track. All her friends followed behind her. The crowd applauded as she walked the entire oval of the racetrack. Jezebel, Aziz, and Bull gathered around her again, and all three horses raised up on their hind legs and whinnied while the spectators went wild.

Bull looked down at Daisy and caught her eye. "Every once in a while, the clouds clear and your star gets to shine. This is *your* day!"

Daisy looked over at Maribel, who winked at her and smiled.

Daisy and her friends were directed to a viewing area beside the stands where they could watch the races. Jezebel, Abdul-Aziz, and Bull-Arch delighted the crowd, each of them winning their event and the coveted wreath of lush, gorgeous flowers.

Once the races were over, the crowd surrounded Daisy. All her friends and the race fans, both children and adults, waited in a long line to get their pictures taken with her. Daisy's heart was filled with happiness. Just when she thought this day could not possibly get any better, the three horses strode over. They dipped their heads and allowed their wreaths of flowers to slide from their heads down over Daisy's. Without noticing it, one of them accidentally knocked her unicorn horn off and down to the ground.

"Oops, let me get that for you," Clarissa said, bending down to pick up the horn.

Daisy laughed cheerfully. "It's okay," she said softly. "I'm happy just the way I am!"

Acknowledgements

How many people does it take to write a book? One, but that person needs a lot of support along the way.

I offer my sincere gratitude to all who have supported my writing and the artwork I created for the Daisy Starshine series. Most of that support came in the form of repeated, and much needed encouragement. And for that I thank my daughters, as well as my friend and author, Donald Vessey, all whom motivated me to keep going even when I couldn't see light at the end of the tunnel.

I am indebted to each of my editors, Peter Senftleben, Melanie Astaire Witt, Nora Cohen, whose help allowed me to appear an accomplished writer, and to complete a polished story. I am also grateful for the assistance of Felicia Campbell, whose final editing and consultation guided me through the process of publication.

Finally, I am supremely thankful for Tina, my wife. Anyone who writes or is otherwise involved in the creative process—although a seemingly solitary pursuit—appreciates the value of someone who is always with them in the trenches. A person who is there when the clouds of doubt have built themselves into a thunderstorm, as well as when they have momentarily cleared. Tina has always been there in any endeavor I have ever undertaken. Without her, Daisy Starshine would not have come into existence, and her shining star would never have been seen.

About the Author

Mark W. Stevens is a Clinical Psychologist, living and practicing in Southern California. His interest in writing began after being prompted by his youngest daughter, Veronica, who asked that he write down the stories he'd told her and her five sisters while they were growing up so they would have them after he was gone.

Paragraphs grew into short stories, poems, essays, novels, and children's books. Drawing from his work of more than 20 years as a psychologist, Mark's writing is an investigation of human nature in the context of environmental and psycho-emotional challenges.

Now that his daughters have left the roost, Mark and his wife live in a home filled with dogs and cats. When not at the office seeing patients or spending time with family, Mark enjoys drawing, painting, music, travel, nature, and of course, writing.

All of the illustrations in the Daisy Starshine Series were hand drawn by Mark. Daisy prints and merchandise are available for purchase. Get in touch for details: DaisyStarshinePrints@gmail.com.

Other Books in the Daisy Starshine Series

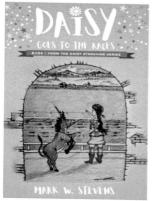  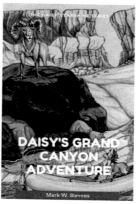

Daisy, a young, orphaned, and disabled donkey, often daydreams of becoming a unicorn. Throughout her adventures, Daisy discovers friendship, courage, and the happiness that comes from accepting yourself as you are.

Lost in The Rainforest

This prequel to *Daisy Goes to the Races*, tells the story of where Daisy came from and how she met Clarissa. After being separated from her family during a severe rainstorm, Daisy becomes lost in a dark and mysterious rainforest. There she discovers Mayan Ruins, encounters fierce predators, and makes wonderful friendships—one of which will last a lifetime.

Daisy's Grand Canyon Adventure

This is a reunion story. When the race season ends, Daisy joins Clarissa and her parents for a vacation to the Grand Canyon. There she braves the rapids of the mighty Colorado River, tangles with a trio of bumbling bank robbers, is guided by mysterious riddle-singing Condors, and stumbles upon a surprise beyond her wildest imagination.

Made in the USA
Columbia, SC
28 October 2022